CHAMPAK

AF653959

The Incredible Hunt

MOONSTONE

Published in Moonstone
by Rupa Publications India Pvt. Ltd 2024
7/16, Ansari Road, Daryaganj
New Delhi 110002

Sales Centres:
Bengaluru Chennai
Hyderabad Jaipur Kathmandu
Kolkata Mumbai Prayagraj

P-ISBN: 978-93-6156-173-3
E-ISBN: 978-93-6156-018-7

First impression 2024

10 9 8 7 6 5 4 3 2 1

Printed in India

Fruit Finder

Simran and Renuka are at the market looking for four seasonal fruits. Read the clues below, and find the fruits that are eaten during the monsoon season.

1. You can eat the hull of two of these fruits and you have to peel the skin to eat the other two.
2. Out of these four fruits, two of them are eaten in the winter season.

Detective Baker!

To celebrate Mother's Day in May, Smita and her friends have made 5 cakes for the cake competition. Read the clues and find the right table where they kept their cakes.

1. Their table has cheesecakes with blueberry and raspberry toppings.
2. Their table is the only one with brown forest cake and pineapple cake.

Flower Map

Neha wants to surprise her mother by getting flowers from her favourite florist. But which one is it? Help Neha find out by reading the clues!

1. The shop is in the middle of the others.
2. There's a watering can near it.
3. The shop stall is painted green

Holi and Seek!

Aryan, Meera, Chetan, and Mansi have made different rangolis to celebra Diwali. Read the hints and find out which rangoli belongs to whom.

1. Aryan has only used red, purple, and yellow colours in his rangoli.
2. Meera has used flowers with colours and also placed diyas in her rangoli
3. Mansi made more than one rangoli, each of which has 4 triangles.

Help Santa's Helper!

Santa gave Elfy the responsibility to deliver 4 sacks of gifts to kids. But Elfy doesn't know which are the right sacks. Read the clues and help Elfy!

1. All the sacks are not kept together.
2. Two sacks have a Christmas symbol on them.
3. Two sacks have the same colour as snow.

Mystery Trip!

World Tourism Day is celebrated on September 27. Zeba just returned from a long foreign trip with her parents. Look at the picture, read the hints and guess which three countries she went to.

1. Zeba went to a historical country where pharaohs lived.
2. She went further down on the African continent and saw Mount Kilimanja
3. She visited an island that shares the same name as an animated movie.

Pick a Look!

October 31 is Halloween. Kuchika wants to go dressed as a wizard, but she is missing a few accessories to complete the costume. Read the hints and examine the picture to find out.

1. When casting a spell, hold me in your hand and flick your wrist.
2. I am white, perched high, and howl at night. Look through me to see clearly as a wizard.
3. An item worn on the head, matching the cloak's colour.

Left or Right?

The World Day of Social Justice is celebrated on February 20. Help Rahul join the right group of protesters.

World Theatre Day is celebrated on March 27. Two groups of kids are performing two different plays. Help Sonu, who is playing a king in one of the plays, reach the correct one.

1. In the play that Sonu is part of, there's a princess and an angel.
2. The princess is wearing a white gown.
3. The play that he is part of does not include a maidservant.

Plant Me Where?

Earth Day is celebrated on April 22. In honour of this day, Ronnie's friends have divided themselves into two groups, performing activities that'll help protect the earth. Based on his preferences, help him choose the correct group.

1. Ronnie loves the environment.
2. Ronnie loves potting plants.
3. Ronnie loves flowers.

Lily's Family!

International Family Day is celebrated on May 15. Four families have gathered together for a celebration. One of the four families is Lily's. Help her find her family.

1. Lily has a baby sister.
2. Lily lives with her grandparents.
3. Lily does not have a brother.

Cake Choice

Help Akhil choose the right cake depending on his taste.

1. Akhil dislikes red cakes.
2. Akhil dislikes fruit cakes.
3. He prefers non-chocolatey cakes.

Crime Solver Charu

Help Charu deliver justice to this man, who has committed a crime.

1. Should she let people bash him for his wrongdoings?
2. Should she take him to court?
3. Should she ask him to admit his crimes beforehand?

This Band or That?

Friendship Day is celebrated every year on the first Sunday of August in many countries, including India. This year it is celebrated on August 4. Help Tannu choose friendship bands for her friends.

1. Tannu likes bands without beads.
2. She likes all colours except brown.
3. She likes stripe and polka patterns

Camera Choosing

World Photography Day is celebrated on August 19. Very recently, Deepa developed a love for photography. Help her choose a camera.

1. She doesn't like to carry heavy cameras.
2. She likes to view the image after clicking it.

Rangoli Racing!

This year, Onam is being celebrated on September 15. Rano wants to participate in the Pookalam Rangoli competition. Help her choose the right group based on her preferences.

1. Rano likes using maroon, orange and white flowers to make the pookalam rangoli.
2. She doesn't like using purple flowers.
3. She likes making flower-shaped rangolis.

A Young Bapu!

To celebrate Gandhi Jayanti on October 2, Mayank has to dress like Mahatma Gandhi for a fancy-dress competition in school. Help him pick the right costume.

Finding Home Alone

On Diwali, Rahul is on his way to meet his friend. Help him spot his friend's house using the clues given below.

1. The house has a colourful rangoli outside it.
2. There are diyas around the rangoli.
3. There is a marigold toran at the main door.

Gifts in Budget!

Shyam has Rs. 300 in his wallet. He wants to buy gifts for four members of his family. Read the hints below and identify what items he can buy with this money.

1. Shyam is good at crafts.
2. He likes writing letters.
3. He makes beautiful cards.

Guide the Scout!

Pooja is looking for her scout leader. Help her reach the right team using the clues given below.

1. The scout leader is wearing a blue scarf.
2. Her scout group's symbol is an eagle.
3. The scout leader's whistle has a cord.

Confused Curie

At her school's science lab, Radha is searching for the correct combination of chemicals and equipment based on the provided clues to perform her experiment.

1. Radha needs a red-coloured chemical and a blue-coloured chemical with a glass stopper on both.
2. She needs two test tubes for the experiment.

A Rose in Need!

Monu is dressing up as Chacha Nehru for Children's Day at his school. But he needs a rose to complete his costume and is at the flower market to buy it. Help him find the rose seller.

1. The florist is sitting next to the marigold seller.
2. He is reading a newspaper.
3. There is a goods truck parked near his stall.

Reading Dilemma!

April 23 is World Book Day. Sudhir wants to read a book, but he's confused. Help him choose a book based on the clues given below.

1. Sudhir does not like reading books that are very thick.
2. He likes reading mysteries and thrillers.
3. He likes books with animals in them.

Dreamy Ice-Creams

Ketan wants to grab a scoop of ice cream on a hot summer afternoon. Use the clues given below to find which stall he should buy his ice-cream from.

1. He wants to have ice cream in a cone.
2. He likes seasonal fruit-flavoured ice cream.
3. He likes to add sprinkles and cherries to his ice cream.

Blood Clues

June 14 is World Blood Donor Day. Sahil has come to a blood donation camp with his mother. Use the hints given below to find out which of the following people will be eligible to donate blood.

1. The donor's haemoglobin level must be more than 12.5%.
2. The donor must be over 18 years of age and weigh more than 50 kg.
3. The donor should not suffer from diabetes, hypertension, cardiac arrest or kidney ailments.

Mangoland!

The International Mango Festival is held from July 9–10. Khushi is learning about the different types of mangoes at the festival. Find out which mangoes are Khushi's favourites using the clues given below.

1. Khushi's favourite mangoes are green-coloured.
2. Her favourite mangoes are available in the month of June.
3. They are grown in West Bengal.

House Trouble!

Maya is trying to figure out which house she belongs to. Use the hints given to help her reach her house on time before the parade starts.

1. Her house leader is a girl.
2. Her house is represented by a freedom fighter who was also a poet.
3. The house has more girls than boys.

Guide Him Home!

August 21 is World Senior Citizens Day. Aryan, the community helper, is guiding the old man, who has lost his way to his home due to his forgetfulness. With the clues that the man gives, help Aryan reach him at his house.

1. The man's house has a red roof.
2. His house has a balcony with flowers and plants.
3. He loves growing vegetables.

Celebrating Ma'am!

Help Ms. Lakshmi reach the correct classroom for Teacher's Day which is celebrated on September 5. Use the hints given in the box.

1. Ms. Lakshmi loves white roses.
2. The blackboard has 'Happy Teacher's Day' written on it.
3. A boy and a girl are standing by the door of her classroom.

Bapu's Teachings

Gandhi Jayanti is celebrated on October 2. Students at a school are unhappy and have decided to stand up for their rights. Help Zoya choose the correct group that highlights Gandhian values and principles to put forward their rights.

1. 2 boys and 2 girls should be in the group.
2. The banner reflects all Gandian values.

Bank Blank!

World Savings Day is celebrated on October 30. Saurav has saved money in his piggy bank. Guide him to the right counter.

1. There's a man behind the counter that Saurav has to go to.
2. There's a small boy standing in front of the counter.
3. Saurav doesn't have to go to the 'Loans' counter.
4. There is no girl standing in front of the counter.

What's the Right Right?

Constitution Day is celebrated on November 26. Piva is dressed up as Babasaheb Ambedkar, the Father of our Constitution, for a fancy dress competition. She has to choose the right article given in the Constitution of India.

Tea Spree!

International Tea Day is celebrated on December 15. Juhi's parents prefer drinking different kinds of tea. With the clues given below, choose the correct tea that her parents would like to drink.

1. Her mom wants her tea to be mixed with spices.
2. Her dad wants his tea to be strong.

Listen to the Farmers!

National Farmers' Day is celebrated on December 23. Choose the group that is making the right demands.

Valentine Dining!

Mr. Mouse is taking Mrs. Mouse out for a Valentine's Day dinner. He has asked the restaurant manager to reserve a special table for them based on Mrs. Mouse's preferences. Find out which table has been reserved for them

1. Mrs. Mouse loves flowers.
2. Mrs. Mouse's favourite food is cheese.
3. Mrs. Mouse likes to start her meal with a dessert.
4. Mr. Mouse had requested a heart-shaped balloon.

Get, Set, Kayak!

Manav is at a kayaking competition. His friend, Nand, is waiting for him. Help Manav find Nand.

1. Nand is wearing a cap.
2. He is carrying a camera in his hand.
3. He is talking to a member of the Red Team.

Library Launchpad

Lisa wants to go to the library to attend a book launch. Help her find the library with the given clues.

1. The library has a ramp.
2. Lisa's friend, Anoop, is waiting for her outside the library.
3. Lisa likes to read science books.

Ride & Seek!

Abhi is at an amusement park. He has won a ticket for a ride. Find out which ride he can go on with the help of the clues given.

1. The ticket is for a ride for two.
2. Abhi doesn't like getting wet.
3. He doesn't like heights.

Van Hunter

An outside broadcasting (OB) van is a vehicle that is used by journalists to cover live events from the spot. Fina Fox has a great scoop that she has to relay to her studio but she has forgotten which OB van is hers. Help her find it.

1. The van is parked next to a street lamp.
2. Fina Fox's company logo is a globe.

Fruit Pursuit

Gaurav's father sent him to the market to buy some fruits. But he forgot which variety of fruit he was asked to buy. Find out which fruit he has to buy with the help of the clues given.

1. It is a good source of vitamin C.
2. It is not a citrus fruit.
3. The fruit has only one seed inside.
4. It is smooth to touch.

Bus Chase!

Ria and Sam have decided to go to school together. Sam has asked Ria to meet him at the bus stop. But their street has 4 bus stops. Using the clues given below, help Ria identify the bus stop where Sam will meet her.

1. They need to catch bus 2A to go to school.
2. The bus stop is usually not crowded.
3. There is an advertisement for chocolates at the bus stop.

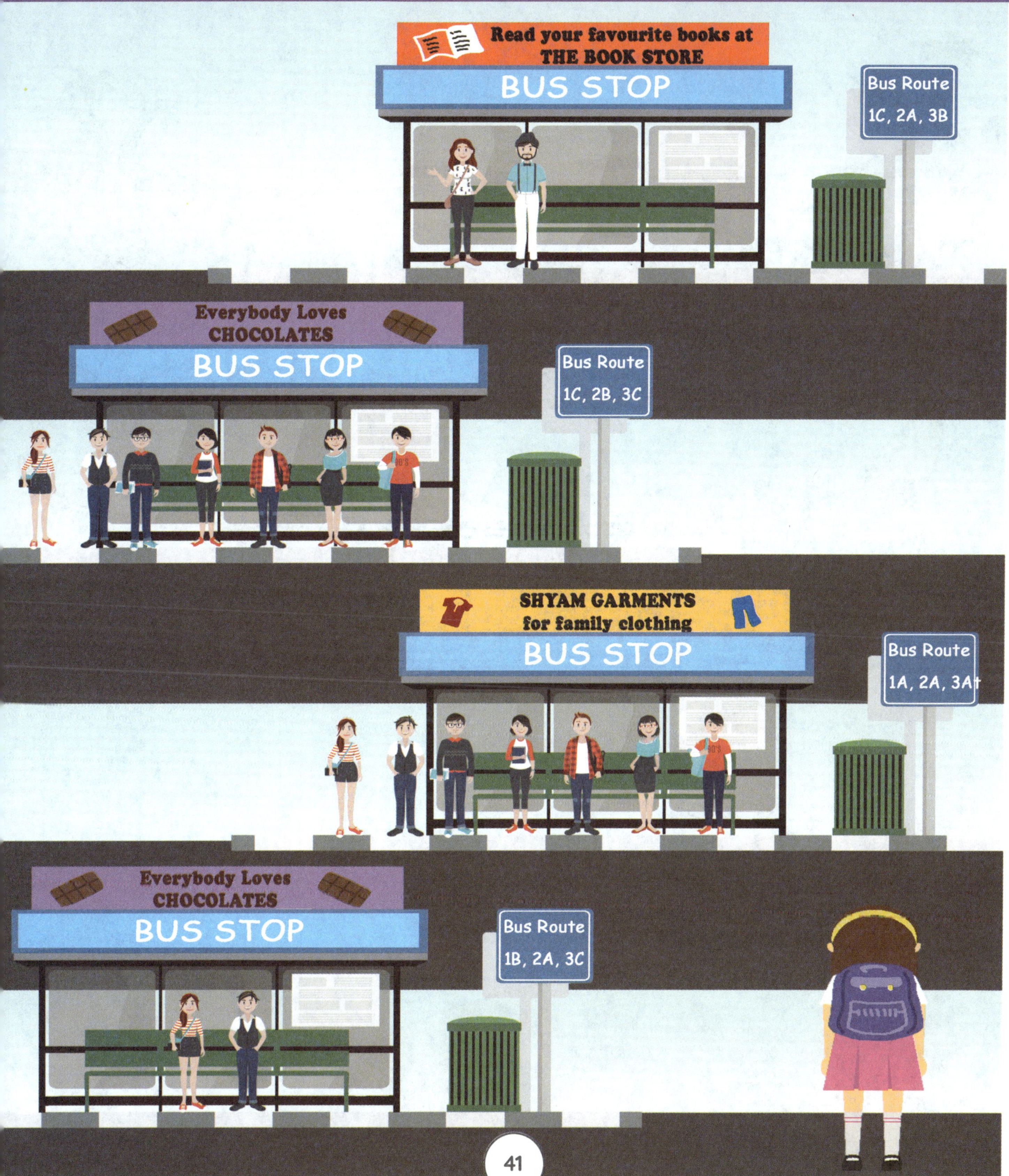

Rowing Race

Shankar is participating in the Onam Snake Boat Race this year. He has decided to meet his team members directly at the river bank. Help him get to his boat in time for the race.

1. His team's boat is decorated with white flowers.
2. His team's uniform is yellow in colour.
3. His boat's number is an even number.

Jeepers Finders!

Wildlife Week is celebrated from October 2nd to 8th in India. Sudha is going on a safari to celebrate it. She is confused about the jeep she's supposed to board. Help her find the jeep using the clues given below:

1. The jeep she's supposed to board has an open top.
2. The jeep doesn't have a camouflage print.
3. She's going on a tiger safari.

Arcade Invader

Soham is at the video game arcade to play his favourite game, Space Invaders. Help him find out which machine is the right one.

1. The game can be played on a blue machine.
2. The machine has no joystick.
3. Buttons and the machine are of the same colour.

Zozo's Bizarre Adventure

Zozo, the alien, is lost and wants to return to his home planet. Help Zozo find his home.

1. Zozo's home planet is blue in colour.
2. His planet has three rings.
3. His planet has two moons.

Scout the Jockey!

Shyam is the studio manager at a radio station. Help him find Manu, the radio jockey.

1. Manu is in the recording studio, interviewing a guest.
2. He is wearing a yellow t-shirt.
3. The person he is interviewing is holding an award.

Flower Map

Help Pratik reach his favourite author's session.

1. The author is seated with one other panelist on stage.
2. There is a camera crew at his session.
3. The talk is meant for children.

Blue's Clues

On World Autism Day, monuments around the world are lit up in blue. This year, electrician Pinto has been told to light up a monument. But he's forgotten which one. Help him identify the monument he has to light up.

1. This monument was not built by the British.
2. It is not a memorial.
3. It is a landmark of Indian independence.

Back to School...?

All the schools in Champakvan have reopened after the summer holidays. Jumpy can't wait to go to school! But which school does he go to?

1. There's a coconut tree right next to Jumpy's school
2. There's a school bus parked at his school.
3. Jumpy will be able to have fun on the school's slide.

Artist's Question

Blacky Bear is in an art class. He has forgotten his canvas. Help him find it using the clues given below:

1. Blacky remembers not painting a portrait.
2. He used paint tubes.
3. He remembers using a lot of black paint.

Row, Row the Boat!

Find the winners using the clues given below.

1. The members of the winning team are wearing blue uniforms.
2. Their oars have red ribbons tied to them.
3. The members of the winning team are wearing sunglasses.

Confusing Class

Ms. Maya has forgotten which class she is supposed to go to. Help her find out using the clues given below.

1. There is a flowerpot outside the classroom.
2. The classroom is on the first floor.
3. The class celebrated a student's birthday the previous day.

Pilot Papa!

Rahul's father is an Indian Air Force pilot. He had given Rahul three clues to help him identify which aircraft he is flying during the airshow. Help Rahul spot his father's aircraft.

1. The aircraft is green in colout.
2. Rahul's father is in a fighter jet.
3. The aircraft has green smoke.

Camper Seeker!

Priyank is at the top of a mountain and is looking down at the campers. Help him spot his friend Pranay's tent. The house has a colourful rangoli.

1. Pranay's tent has a stripe design.
2. His tent is near the lake.
3. There is a bonfire lit outside the tent.

Cruising Crisis!

Grandma and Grandpa are going on a cruise. Help them find the yacht they need to board with the help of the clues given below.

1. The yacht's name has a Roman numeral.
2. The yacht has a sail.
3. The captain is standing on the yacht.

Pick a Cake!

Rahul's mother has sent him to the bakery to buy a Christmas cake. Help him choose the right cake using the clues given below.

1. Mom does not like chocolate cakes.
2. Rahul's sister has specifically asked for cherries on the cake.
3. Rahul loves reindeer.

Find a Friend!

Shahid has been invited to his friend Rohan's house for a birthday party. But, while he is on the right street, he has forgotten which house Rohan lives in. Can you help Shahid find the house he has to go to?

1. The house is decorated with balloons.
2. The house is decorated with streamers.
3. The house has a striped roof.

Mystery at the Exhibit!

Samir is at a technology exhibition. He was supposed to meet his friend, Rajiv here. Can you help him find Rajiv based on the clues given below?

1. Raijv didn't bring anything with him.
2. He is fascinated by the defence services.
3. He's wearing a green t-shirt.

Secret Admirer!

Zain has received an anonymous Valentine's Day card asking him to meet his secret admirer. Help Zain find his admirer using the clues given below.

1. I will be holding a red flower.
2. I will be waiting near a fountain.
3. I have a flowery pattern on my skirt.

Detective Baker!

Katie, the caterpillar, has to meet her cousin Bianca, the butterfly, in the park. But Bianca was only a caterpillar when Katie last saw her. Can you help her identify Bianca based on the clues given?

1. Bianca likes to be near red flowers.
2. Bianca likes to read books.
3. Bianca has the same pattern on her wings as Katie has on her back.

Door-full Dream!

Joshua is having a dream where he is stuck in a room with many doors, but only one of them will wake him up. Can you help him find the right door to lead him out? Below are some clues that he remembers about the door.

1. It has a pattern on it.
2. It is not a rectangle.
3. It is hard to reach.

Quest for the Poets!

Shirin has to go attend her friend's poetry recital at a community arts festival. Can you help her find her way to the poetry recital area using only the clues provided?

1. The poetry recital area has a microphone and a small stage.
2. The poetry recital area would be in a quiet area, not near any loud sources of sound.
3. The poetry recital area would have seats for the audience to sit down.

Island Finder!

The island has no saltwater crocodiles on it.

1. The island has mangrove trees on it that have blue-green leaves.
2. The island does not have any man-made constructions on it.

Zoo Day Out!

Harpreet has gone to the zoo with her family. They all separated to see what they wanted, and agreed to meet at one common place. Can you help her find that place?

1. The spot is beyond the snake exhibit but not as far as the ape exhibit.
2. The spot is close to the food in case they get hungry, and seating in case they get tired.
3. The spot is far from the lion cages.

Uniform Trouble!

Peter had to go meet his father after school, but everyone who works here looks alike in their uniform. Thankfully, Peter's father had given him some clues about where he'd be waiting for him. Can you help Peter find his father?

1. Peter's father is carrying a red tiffin box.
2. Peter's father takes a scooter to work, so he will be near the scooter parking.
3. Peter's father is called Skyscraper by his friends because he is taller than most of them.

Flower Power!

Benny Bee's friend Bobby had told him of a flower with very sweet nectar in this garden. Can you help him find where it is?

1. The flower is near the sunflowers, but is not a sunflower.
2. The flower has a caterpillar one one of its leaf.
3. The flower has pointy petals, not round ones.

Answer

Page 1

Page 2

Page 3

Page 4

Aryan's *rangoli* : A
Meera's *rangoli* : C
Mansi's *rangoli* : B & E
Chetan's *rangoli* : D

Page 5

Page 6

Zeba went to Egypt, Tanzania and Madagascar.

Page 7

Page 8

Page 9

Page 10

Page 11

Page 12

Page 13

Page 14

Page 15

Page 16

Answer

Page 17

Page 18

Page 19

Page 20

Page 21

Page 22

Page 23

Page 24

Page 25

Page 26

Page 27

Page 28

Page 29

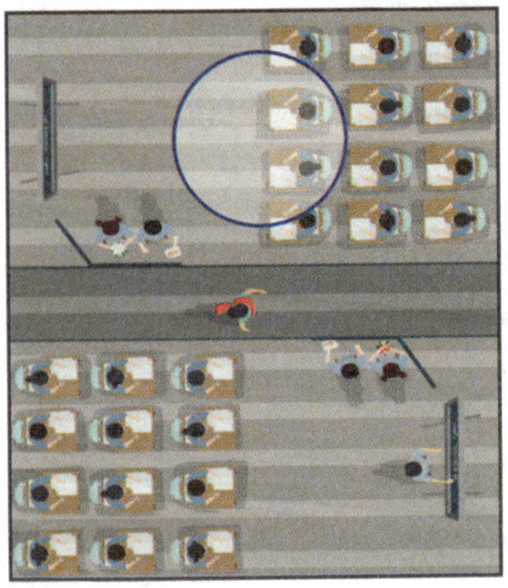

Page 30

Page 31

Page 32

Answer

Page 33

Page 34

Page 35

Page 36

Page 37

Page 38

Page 39

Page 40

Page 41

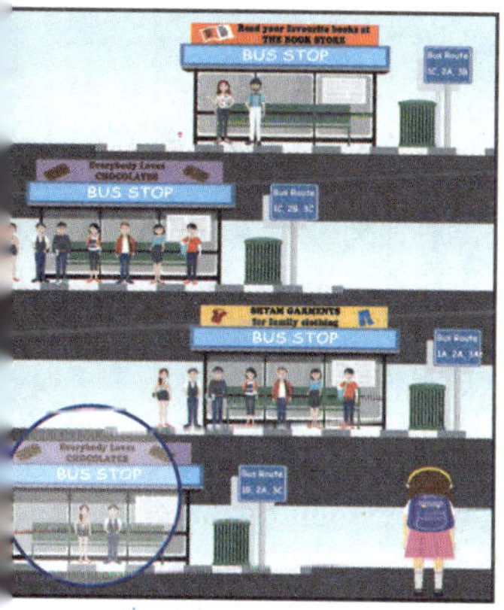

Page 42

Page 43

Page 44

Page 45

Page 46

Page 47

Page 48

Answer

Page 49

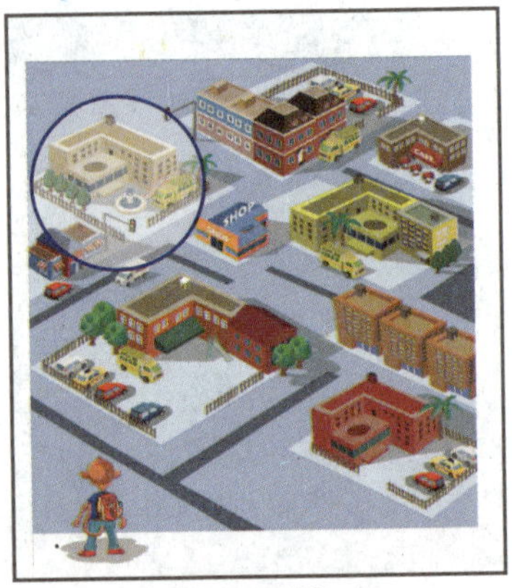

Page 50

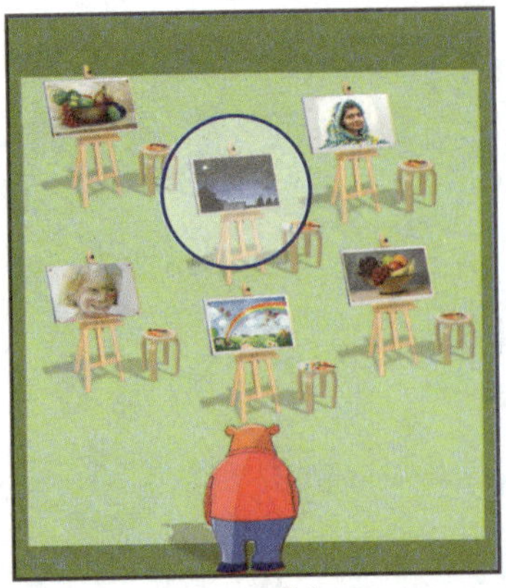

Page 51

Page 52

Page 53

Page 54

Page 55

Page 56

Page 57

Page 58

Page 59

Page 60

Page 61

Page 62

Page 63

Page 64

Page 65

Page 66